A Richard Jackson Book

Dreamplace

by GEORGE ELLA LYON
paintings by PETER CATALANOTTO

Orchard Books   New York

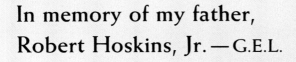

In memory of my father,
Robert Hoskins, Jr.—G.E.L.

For my sister Nancy—P.C.

Special thanks to Bobbie, Maddie, Whitney, and especially Fiona—P.C.

Text copyright © 1993 by George Ella Lyon
Illustrations copyright © 1993 by Peter Catalanotto
First Orchard Paperbacks edition 1998

Orchard Books, 95 Madison Avenue, New York, NY 10016

Manufactured in the United States of America. Printed by Barton Press, Inc.
Bound by Horowitz/Rae. Book design by Mina Greenstein
The text of this book is set in 18 point Weiss Bold. The illustrations are watercolor
paintings reproduced in full color.
Hardcover   10   9   8   7   6   5   4   3
Paperback   10   9   8   7   6   5   4   3   2   1

Library of Congress Cataloging-in-Publication Data
Lyon, George Ella, date. Dreamplace / by George Ella Lyon ; paintings by Peter
Catalanotto.   p.   cm. Summary: Present-day visitors describe what they see when they visit
the pueblos where the Anasazi lived long ago.
ISBN 0-531-05466-7. (tr.)   ISBN 0-531-08616-X (lib. bdg.)   ISBN 0-531-07101-4 (pbk.)
[1. Pueblo Indians—Fiction.   2. Indians of North America—Southwest, New—Fiction.]
I. Catalanotto, Peter, ill.   II. Title.   PZ7.L9954Dr   1993   [E]—dc20   92-25102

We drive up a steep road,
hike a paved trail
among yucca, pinyon, juniper
and tourists.

It's all plain as beans
till we come around a bend

and see for the first time
across the trees:

like a dream, like a sandcastle
this city the Pueblo people built under a cliff.

Towers and courtyards,
hearths and kivas
hung where the eagle nests.

A sandcastle, but no water—

every drop carried down from mesa
or up from canyon
to this place

where the Anasazi
                    sang
                        and danced
                            and prayed

plaited sandals, wove baskets,
coiled clay into pots.

Food, too,
had to be grown above them
or hunted below them

harvest and kill
borne home on their backs

hands
        and
feet
        finding
slots
        in the
stone.

In the courtyards, they took *mano*,
rounded pounding stones,
and crushed the corn into meal
on flat stones, *metate*,

and fed their families for a hundred years

as evening stretched its hand

over the mesa

and bathed their dwelling for a moment
in pink light.

Then

water dried up
corn withered
sickness came.

They packed their prayer sticks and grinding stones
climbed down the cliff face

and set off

leaving us

far in the future

to drive up roads they never knew

and hike trails to their city
and stand amazed

at the people
who built this dream
who lit its walls
with fire and stories

and then one day
when even trees were hungry
turned their backs

and let it go.